Have a
Wonderful
Birthday
Love Grandma &
Grandpa
Kreighbaum
Uncle Josiah

Dorothy AND TOTO

What's YOUR Name?

by Debbi Michiko Florence

illustrated by Monika Roe

PICTURE WINDOW BOOKS
a capstone imprint

Wizard of Oz: Dorothy and Toto
is published by Picture Window Books,
a Capstone Imprint
1710 Roe Crest Drive
North Mankato, Minnesota 56003
www.mycapstone.com

CAPS34782

Library of Congress Cataloging-in-Publication Data
Names: Florence, Debbi Michiko, author.
Title: Dorothy and Toto. What's your name? /
by Debbi Michiko Florence.
Other titles: What's your name? | What is your name?
Description: North Mankato, Minnesota : Picture Window
Books, a Capstone imprint, [2016] | Series: Warner
Brothers. Dorothy and Toto | Summary: Dorothy tries to
find a way to tell her new Munchkin friend, Milton, that
she does not like being called by nicknames.
Identifiers: LCCN 2016011090| ISBN 9781479587025
(library binding) | ISBN 9781479587063 (paperback) |
ISBN 9781479587100 (ebook (pdf))
Subjects: LCSH: Gale, Dorothy (Fictitious character)—
Juvenile fiction. | Toto (Fictitious character) Juvenile
fiction. | Nicknames—Juvenile fiction. | CYAC:
Nicknames—Fiction. | Friendship—Fiction.
Classification: LCC PZ7.1.F593 Dt 2016 | DDC [Fic]—dc23
LC record available at http://lccn.loc.gov/2016011090

Designer: Alison Thiele
Editor: Jill Kalz

illustrated by Monika Roe

Printed in China.

007729

Table of Contents

Chapter 1
A New Friend 5

Chapter 2
Lots of Names 11

Chapter 3
Help from Friends 19

Chapter 4
A Dog Named Toto 27

Chapter 5
My Name Is Dorothy 33

Chapter 1

A New Friend

Dorothy Gale and her dog, Toto, live in the Land of Oz. Each day brings a surprise. Each day is a fun adventure.

One sunny morning, Dorothy and Toto went exploring. They walked through the woods. Then they came to a pond.

A Munchkin boy stood in the water.

(Munchkins are small, friendly people.)

He held a fishing pole.

"Good morning," Dorothy said.

"Hello," said the Munchkin.

"My name is Dorothy Gale. What is your name?"

"Everyone calls me Milty," the Munchkin said.

"It is very nice to meet you, Milty," Dorothy said. "We are exploring. This is my dog —"

Dorothy looked down, but Toto wasn't there. He was chasing a squirrel.

"Oh! Silly dog," Dorothy said. "I'm sorry, Milty. I have to go. See you later!"

"Goodbye, Doro," Milty said.

Dorothy ran after Toto. She followed him to a large tree.

"I think the squirrel got away, Toto," she said.

Toto wagged his tail.

"I wonder why Milty called me Doro," she said. "I told him my name is Dorothy."

Toto barked.

"I'm sure he will call me by my name next time," Dorothy said.

But Milty had more new names for Dorothy the following day.

Chapter 2

Lots of Names

"Good morning, Milty!" Dorothy called. "What are you doing?"

"Hello, Dot!" the Munchkin said. "I'm picking apples. Would you like some apples?"

"Yes, please," Dorothy said.

Milty picked three apples and gave
them to Dorothy. "I have to hurry
home now," he said. "I'm baking pies.
See you later, Dotty!"

"Goodbye, Milty," Dorothy said. "Thank you!"

Dorothy hugged Toto. "Milty is very kind," she said. "But I wish he would call me Dorothy."

Toto licked Dorothy's cheek.

Later that day, Dorothy looked for pretty stones. She liked the pink ones best. Milty passed by on his bicycle.

"Good afternoon, Little D!" Milty called to her.

Dorothy waved and smiled. "My name is Dorothy," she said quietly. She did not say it loud enough for Milty to hear.

Every time Dorothy saw Milty, he called her a different name.

Lotsa Dots.

Dor-dor.

Dee.

Dotty Dooly.

Dorothy was afraid to ask Milty to call her by her real name. Maybe his feelings would be hurt. Maybe he wouldn't want to talk to her anymore.

Toto pawed at Dorothy's leg.

"You're right, Toto," Dorothy said.
"When you have a problem, it's good
to ask for help. Let's invite our friends
over tomorrow."

Chapter 3

Help from Friends

The next day, Scarecrow, Tin Man, and the Cowardly Lion came to Dorothy's house. They all drank milk and ate cookies.

"I need your help," Dorothy said. "I have a new friend. His name is Milty. He is very nice, but he never calls me by my name."

"Did you TELL him your name?" Scarecrow asked.

"Yes, I did," Dorothy said.

"Maybe you said your name too quietly," Scarecrow said. "Maybe he didn't hear you."

"Perhaps," Dorothy said. "He calls me other names. Like Dot or Little D."

"He must like you," Tin Man said. "Those are nice nicknames."

The Cowardly Lion shared his cookie with Toto. "Maybe he's too shy to say your real name," he said.

"What should I do?" Dorothy asked.

Scarecrow smiled. "I don't think this is a problem, Dorothy."

"Oh, but it is!" Dorothy cried. "What if I called you Scaredycrow instead of Scarecrow? What if I called Tin Man Tinny? Or Lion Fuzzy?"

The Cowardly Lion gripped his tail. "I do not like the name Fuzzy," he said.

Tin Man shook his head. "I do not like the name Tinny," he said.

"Tell Milty your name again," Scarecrow said. "That sounds like the best idea to me."

"Don't do it, Dorothy," Lion said. "You might hurt his feelings. He might stop being your friend."

THAT'S what troubled Dorothy most. She didn't want to lose a friend. Maybe it was better to say nothing. "Oh, dear," she said.

Scarecrow gave Dorothy a hug. "You are brave, nice, and smart," he said. "You will find a time to tell Milty how you feel."

"I'm sure he will still want to be your friend," Tin Man said.

Dorothy hoped they were right.

Chapter 4

A Dog Named Toto

A few days later, Dorothy saw Milty again. She was reading a book to Toto.

"Hello, Polka Dot!" Milty said. "Can I listen too?"

Dorothy wanted to speak up and tell Milty her name. But instead she said, "Yes, please sit with us, Milty."

When Dorothy finished reading, Milty clapped. Dorothy wanted to

thank him for being her friend. She wanted to tell him her name. But instead she said, "I'm glad you liked the story."

"I'm glad we're friends, Doodle Noodle," Milty said.

Toto wagged his tail.

"Your dog is cute," Milty said. "May I pet him?"

"Yes," Dorothy said. "He is very, very friendly."

Milty pet Toto. "Your dog is so soft!" he said. "What is his name?"

"Toto," Dorothy said.

"Hello, Toto," Milty said.

Toto spun in a circle.

"He likes that you called him by his name," Dorothy said. "He likes to be called Toto."

Milty nodded. "I know how he feels," he said. "My friends call me Milty, but my real name is Milton."

"Oh! Your real name is Milton?" Dorothy asked.

"It is," Milty said.

Dorothy remembered Scarecrow's words: *You will find a time to tell Milty how you feel.* Now was the perfect time. She knew just what to say.

Chapter 5

My Name Is Dorothy

Dorothy smiled. She asked, "Do you wish your friends called you Milton instead of Milty?"

"I do," Milty said. "Milty is a nice nickname. But it's not as nice as my real name."

"I know how you feel," Dorothy said. "Doro, Dee, and Polka Dot are nice nicknames. But they're not as nice as my real name."

Toto barked and jumped.

"I have an idea," Dorothy said. "I will call you Milton if you call me Dorothy. That is my name, and I like it best."

"That's a great idea!" Milton said. "Hello, Dorothy."

"Hello, Milton," Dorothy said.

Milton bowed. "Pleased to meet you, Dorothy. And Toto too."

"We're pleased to meet YOU, Milton," Dorothy said.

Milton patted Toto's head.

"Dorothy, we should call Toto 'TooToo,'" he said. "He looks like a

TooToo, doesn't he?"

Toto's tail drooped. Dorothy tried to hide her smile.

"Oh, I'm kidding, Toto!" Milton said. "I will always call you Toto."

Toto yipped. Dorothy and Milton laughed. They were happy friends in the Land of Oz.

About The Wizard of Oz

The Wizard of Oz follows young Dorothy Gale and her little dog, Toto, who are magically taken by tornado from Kansas to the Land of Oz. Dorothy sets off on the Yellow Brick Road and meets Scarecrow, Tin Man, and the Cowardly Lion. They join her on a dangerous journey to meet the Wizard of Oz, whose powers may help Dorothy return home.

The Wizard of Oz is one of the most beloved stories of all time. The book was written by L. Frank Baum and published in 1900. It was made into a movie starring Judy Garland in 1939.

Glossary

cowardly (KOW-erd-lee) — not brave

droop (DROOP) — to hang down

invite (in-VITE) — to ask to do something

nickname (NICK-name) — a name used instead of someone's real name

perfect (PER-fekt) — without a problem or mistake

Use Your Brain

1. Milton calls Dorothy "Doro" and "Dot." What other nicknames does he give her?

2. Why won't Dorothy tell Milton how she feels about the nicknames?

3. Dorothy is a very kind person. Give examples of things she says or does that show her kindness.

About the Author

Debbi Michiko Florence writes books for kids and teens in The Word Nest, her writing studio that overlooks a pond. Her work includes two nonfiction books for kids and a chapter book series, Jasmine Toguchi. Debbi is a California native who currently lives in Connecticut with her husband, her little dog, and two ducks. She loves to travel around the world with her husband and daughter. Before she became an author, Debbi volunteered as a raptor rehabilitator and worked as an educator at a zoo.

About the Illustrator

Monika Roe was born with a passion for art. She grew up in a small town on California's central coast and couldn't wait to get to the big city, where she earned a degree in graphic design and entered the world of advertising. She worked as an award-winning art director and creative director in Los Angeles, California, and Indianapolis, Indiana, before becoming a full-time illustrator. Monika's studio is located in the redwood forest of California's Santa Cruz Mountains. There she creates illustrations for people throughout the world while her pug snores loudly in the background.

CHECK OUT MORE
Dorothy
AND
TOTO
ADVENTURES!

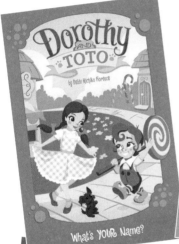

What's YOUR Name?

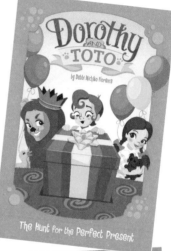

The Hunt for the Perfect Present

The Disappearing Picnic

Little Dog Lost

For MORE GREAT BOOKS go to
www.MYCAPSTONE.com